CHE

DEDICATED TO CHE GUEVARA

RT CHIWUTA

Che
Dedicated to Che Guevara

Copyright © 2023 by RT Chiwuta

Paperback ISBN: 978-1-63812-637-9
Ebook ISBN: 978-1-63812-638-6

All rights reserved. No part in this book may be produced and transmitted in any form or by any means, electronic, or mechanical, including photocopying, recording, or by any information storage and retrieval system, without permission in writing from the copyright owner.

The views expressed in this work are solely those of the author and do not necessarily reflect the views of the publisher. It hereby disclaims any responsibility for them.

Published by Pen Culture Solutions   04/24/2023

Pen Culture Solutions
1-888-727-7204 (USA)
1-800-950-458 (Australia)
support@penculturesolutions.com

CHE

The fundamental question is, what is the purpose of human life? Why are we here? Relative to the existence of the individual as a sole entity, then a communal entity and a global entity or even yet a universal entity. Why are we here in the context of being a human being? Why do we suffer, why is there strife, disease, pain, war, human discord and everything else we face? Of course though, life is also beautiful so one should not understate that.

However, certainly the most intriguing philosophical question one can argue is why is there suffering of any kind? For it is visceral, tragic and seems hard to understand. In the context of pursuing a Masters qualification that will be focused on learning the ethical dimensions of the interdependence of collective living on this planet with regards to the issues we face, it seems an important philosophical basis to start from.

Throughout human history, humanity has faced challenges both man made and in the hands of the Gods. We have waged war, conquered and pillaged. We have exploited and enslaved one another and in the 21st century, our ability to kill in the most developed armies of the world is as sophisticated as it has ever been. Concomitant to those challenges and that reality, according to a lot of general consensus, we face the greatest peril of our own making due to global warming caused by how we live as a consequence of industrialisation.

With regards to industrialisation, which has completely transformed life on this planet in truly wondrous ways such that people who lived in the preindustrial world would scarcely believe the world we live in today. Such accelerated progress in just over a century or so. One can conclude that we certainly have the means and ability to affect our lives in a positive way on this planet. The power is in our hands. The question then is, how do we get past all that's in the way? The complex politics, beliefs and human limitations that lead to discord. What is our obligation to one another from the very basic level to the planetary level?

The above is a draft I wrote when I was applying for my Masters in Ethics and Global justice. I thought it would be apt to include it at the beginning of my book as it reflects in a significant way what I believe to be my raison detre which I am trying to fulfil.

This, hence, leads into why I tilted the book Che after Che Guevara and why the initial poem will be about him. In the first instance, I am inspired by people who come and live great lives. Lives with purpose and leave a mark on our collective consciousness. Especially people who are led by conscience and try and influence positive social change for the masses at great sacrifice or in the face of significant danger and repudiation by oppressive forces. A lot of these people came in the last century and yesteryear because a lot of work needed to be done and, in my opinion, Che Guevara was one of these people. I remember growing up and Che Guevara T shirts were ubiquitous and seemed to be the fashion item of choice for the socially conscious. For me it demonstrates that he captured the imagination of a Zeitgeist. People got his intention and drive. A man who was so moved by the poverty he saw that he fought till his dying day those he saw as responsible when he could have chosen to live a life of privilege and indifference. He was after all from a privileged background. Hence its truly inspiring the empathy of the man. Imagine if we all had just a little bit of Che in us.

This book is a continuation of my journey of poetic self-expression which has been accidental and unintentional. I have been writing since my early twenties but I still do not consider myself a writer and the urge to write only occurs as an epiphany. As did my last book Ottilie Rose. Once that was concluded, I did not see myself writing for a long time. However, the poem Che came into my mind after one day being curious to learn more about him as I am curious to learn so much but there is so much to learn and not enough time. So, I wrote it and again did not think it meant anything and certainly wasn't the beginning of another collection. At the very least I was looking at years before I could compile poetry to equate to another book. However, here I am roughly eight months later having amassed another collection. I am now sitting to edit it and read the poems and I will be reading it just as you will be, as a discovery for I will admit. These poems are not mine. I am only a scribe. Hence, once received I read them from a position of not knowing, not remembering and most importantly as I stated afore, discovery. I at the very least, just have a vocabulary good enough to be a good recipient of the of the words.

Consequently, I hope the reader can enjoy and most importantly, discover something for themselves. The poetry itself as in all my books is discursive and meandering just like my brain. Hope this will be a cause of enjoyment for the reader rather than anything else. Lastly, as in my preceding collection, Ottilie Rose, the poems are written and dated in the date order they were received and scribed.

And so it goes…

25/4/22

Che Guevara,
What a man you were,
What a life you lived,
Some come and go,
Leave this earthly plane without a whimper,
But yours was one of the greatest lives lived,
Born of purpose,
Born with a purpose,
You stayed steadfast to the goals of transformation,
You fought with your heart,
You fought with your mind,
You fought with guns,
Fighting for the lowest of the low,
So they too could be raised,
You saw unfairness and injustice as a stain on humanity,
And you dedicated your life to see an end to it,
But that fight was more than one man can win,
For human existence is complex,
You were not afraid to kill,
And for some that's a step too far,
Yet the realities of life mean killing is a part of life,
And for this you showed you were indeed just human too,
And faced by those willing to kill to have their way in the world,
What is a man to do?
How many amongst us would so resolutely give their life to struggle?
Be so moved by the circumstances of the most unfortunate amongst us,
Be so willing to shift the world for them,
No one person has the answer to all the world's problems,
No one person's ideas can account for it all,
But your commitment that it should be better,
Was greater than so many put together,
Some come to this mortal plane and leave without a whimper,

And yet, some come and live a life's experience worth multiple life times,
In only thirty nine short years you did this,
You saw imperialism as a blight on humanity,
Racism too,
You cared deeply,
This even your detractors cannot deny,
Some come and go without a whimper,
And yet some come and are called to be great,
Some are called to be the greatest,
You were one of the greatest,
For your life and your passion put against those of most,
None can match,
You were one of the greatest,
And you were great,
If the possibility of the fairer world you fought for could somehow be realised,
The spirit of it,
What a world it would be.

7/7/22

Love is a beautiful thing,
And when it is found,
It is a precious thing,
A truly precious thing,
Kindred spirits,
Friends,
Best friends,

You are and become,
Cherish it you must,

For not many things in this life can provide the comfort and refuge that a truly loving relationship can,
Nurture it for like a garden,

It must constantly be tended to from the pests, the weeds, the thorns,

It must be watered with kindness

Else like the plants in the garden without water,

It will and they do, wither and die,
A truly precious thing it is,
And may those who have found love have more happy days than sad days,
For richer or for poorer they say,
For richer or for poorer.

19/7/22

It was almost perfect,
They say perfection doesn't exist,
But it was almost perfect,
Matched in so many ways,
A transcendent connection,
A powerful connection,
A real connection,
It seemed meant to be,
It was almost perfect,
They say perfection doesn't exist,
Perhaps that's why it couldn't be,
Because it was almost perfect,
We almost had it all,
But alas it slipped through our grasp,
It wasn't meant to be,
But it was almost perfect,
We almost had it all,
But it wasn't meant to be,
Alas,
It was almost perfect,

To all those who have loved and lost,

Just know you fought the good fight,

But never be jaded,

Always believe in love and in greater possibilities,

Go through the pain,

Then love again,

It's the only fight in this life really worth having.

20/7/22

Sing song bird sing,
Fly free bird fly,
Fly,
Fly high,
Touch the sky,
Fly beyond the sky,
Fly to the edge of the universe,
Touch infinity,
Touch the very edge of space,
Embrace possibility,
Embrace it all,
Embrace opportunity,
Embrace the opportunity to be,
Sing song Bird,
Fly free Bird,
You are free no,
Gone are the shackles,
Gone are the chains,
The only chains left,
Are the chains of your self-imposed limitations,
You have much to strive for,
Much to fight for,
A brutal legacy to overcome,
A brutal legacy to reinvent,
This is your destiny,
Sing song Bird,
Fly free bird,
For you are free.

23/7/22

One day it seemed our paths were destined to cross,
As if the universe played a trick and the stars aligned,
So your life and mine could become one,
Yet only a trick it seems,
For we went our separate ways,
Another illusion like the infinite illusions in the universe,
The ultimate illusionist,
The Universe,
Nothing is quite what it seems,
Things that seem harmless,
Will kill,
Even things that seem beautiful,
Will mangle, poison and destroy,
The beauty and the beast,
You miss what you had when love is lost,
You experience the beauty of falling in love,
Then the beast of going asunder,
You miss them,
You miss love,
You miss loving,
Even miss fighting for love,
You just miss,
Yet it feels beautiful to drink the sadness,
Drink from the cup of sorrow,
The cup of longing,
What strange magic.

26/7/22

To new things,
The past,
Like a haze,
It hovers,
Like a mirage,
Blurring the line between reality and imagination,
As you cling on to things that were,
But can never again be,
Hard to let go,
Especially the fond memories,
The great dreams and aspirations,
The great possibilities that once fuelled insatiable passions,
But alas were never fulfilled,
Leaving a great big hole,
A void in the lived experience,

A vacuum,

Nothingness,

A black hole,

Which makes it difficult to escape the misery,
Difficult to let things go,
Difficult to let go of the past,
And look to the future,
Or better yet,
Appreciate and accept the present,
So it's to new things one must look,
Not that new will be better,
But that new could be better,
Especially in times of loss,
Times of moaning,
Times of renewal,
Nature teaches it best,

With each new sunrise,
Brings a new day,
New possibilities,
New eventualities,
New renewal,
So to new things I say,
To new things.

Steve Biko,
The great souls,
The great souls that come and visit amongst us,
Us mere mortals,
Those called to great purpose,
To face the greatest challenges,
How to free a captured people,
At the risk of death,
You were one such soul,
Question being,
What world do we live in that you should meet the end you did?
Bruised and beaten,
On a cold prison floor,
What is it about this world,
That those with the purest intent,
Seem to meet the most unjust of ends,
And face the most unjust of circumstances,
What is it about this world?
Yet as we fight for a better world,
Say we are trying to make the world a better place,
Were you to come back,
What would you think of today?
Or are the struggles of each generation just a symptom of being alive?
A symptom of living,
A symptom of breathing,
You had yours,
We have ours,
And as you solve old problems,
New ones come and take their place,
And so it goes,
And goes,
And goes,
And it's gone,
And gone,

And gone,
Like a never ending dance,
Swaying left and right,
Left and right,
For eternity ,
Or a never ending song,
The same song playing forever and ever,
Just with different singers each time,
But it's the same song none the less,
Or the same play,
Just with different actors,

And a slightly different plot each time,

But the basic ingredients the same,
One can only wonder,
If that's all there is for us?

Just repeating the same old mistakes, tales, tragedies and injustices,

For as long as we continue to be,
Or would you come and tell us different Steve,
If you came back and saw what's different in the world,
Compared to the world you were so brutally and callously expelled from,
Maybe you would say,
I couldn't have believed it,
But a different song is possible,
A different play,
And that maybe we can meet the ensuing challenges with hope and not despair,
Maybe that's what you would say Steve.

29/7/22

Che

The sojourn into the realm of the living,
The realm of matter and consequence,
A short journey of many many days,
Where the sun shines and shines and shines,
Life.

14/8/22

The soft embrace of a long lost love,
Memories,
Copious memories,
Days of gentle bliss,
Laughs and giggles,
The warm embrace of true love,
Why did you have to go?
Oh but what memories you left,
That warm feeling in the center of the heart,
Fondness,
Only fondness,
And a belief that it can be found again,
On a quiet uneventful day,
When nostalgia and memories are triggered,
What memories to rekindle,
The memories of a long lost love,
Maybe it's briefness was its glory,
That love,
Maybe time might have ruined it,
But that it was had,
A treasure,
A truly beautiful connection,
Two innocent young lovers,
Curious and playful,
Oh what blissful innocence,
Laughs and smiles,
Laughs and smiles,
And warm embraces,
The warm glow of love,
Mostly what was shared,
Oh to be alive,
And have such moments,
Though fleeting,
Does it not make it all worthwhile?
Despite everything,

Despite it all,
All that threatens to efface the beauty,
Yet today I bask in the soft embrace of a long lost love,
The memories,
The fond memories,
The beauty of the moment,
That can never be taken away,
Universe,
I thank thee.

A different kind of love,
Then there's that love that tests you,
That grows you,
That challenges you,
That puts you under life's microscope,
Maybe even breaks you,
When your hopes are dashed,
Your hopes and dreams are not fulfilled,
Your idealistic aspirations are thwarted,
The love where you persevere and struggle,
Like a child born with an affliction,
Losing a loved one,
Or a relationship that's not working out,
When you truly hope it would have and it should,
That's a different kind of love,
A love where you take lessons, strength and wisdom,
For that's the only real choice you have.

15/8/22

Spinning and spinning,
Through infinite space,
Suspended seemingly in thin air by many miraculous cosmic forces,
Spinning and spinning,
As day turns to night,
And night turns to day,
And so on and so on,
Spinning and spinning,
This so called earth,
Us so called humans,
Living this so called life,
For all it is,
Spinning and spinning,
Earth just spinning and spinning,
I wish I could see the whole picture,
Just for a brief moment,
Know what it was all about,
Not speculate,
But know,
Even for the briefest of moments,
To satisfy my curiosity,
Make it all make sense,
All of it,
Why we even have to be here in the first place,
For all we go through that challenges the senses,
Spinning and spinning,
Spinning and spinning,
Just spinning and spinning.

17/8/2022

Humanity,
The great battle of ideas,
Right and wrong,
Each mind a universe of opinions,
A universe of experiences,
Insights on reality held as fact,
In fact however,
At least, some facts seemingly stand true,
As far as we have been able to establish at least,
Or our intelligence will allow,
To keep the fabric of our reality together,
Else it's all chaos,
Especially in the world of opinions,
The great sea of opinions,
Humanity's tempest,
The real truth however,
Perhaps that's for another day,
Another lifetime,
Another reality.

28/8/22

CHE

Standing by the graveside,
As we honour the memory of the fallen,
Remember them in their living days,
Those who have gone to rest,
Breathed their Last breath,
What of us the living,
How do we make most of the time we still have?
How do we maximise the privilege of the breath?
So we can truly realise what life could truly be.

19/9/22

If life has meaning,
For it all to have meaning,
Then why even lead by the best intentions,
By the seeming guidance of the universe,
God itself and the deepest intuition,
All your endeavours can end in ruin?
The good fall by the wayside,
At the hands of the wicked,
Death upon misery,
And misery upon death,
Pain and solitude,
If life has any meaning,
What's the meaning of it all?
Seemingly to endure,
Endure and endure,
And as we endure is it for this plane or another?
Does it matter?
For endure we must,
That seems to be the deepest lesson,
Just to keep going,
Keep moving,
And never give up,
Maybe the widest view is beyond our view,
So as we ask these questions,
The true answers remain beyond us,
So toil we must,
Endure we must,
No matter what.

16/11/2022

The end of something,
Is the beginning of another,
A new realm,
A new context,
A new paradigm,
A new algorithm of reality,
Whole new possibilities,
Even when we don't want it to end,
Especially when we don't want it to end,
When we fear it ending,
That's the widest space for new possibilities,
It's strange as people with our attachments, commitments and connections,
Random bits of cosmic string,
It could all be completely different but for coincidence and chance,
Chemical alchemy,
But life is greater and grander,
What governs us beyond the perceptible,
Lying in the imperceptible,
All we have is beliefs and probabilities,
Inspired and breath-taking observations and insights,
But to what is really is,
Well, isn't that just the question,
All this to say what's possible is beyond what we can imagine,
Even more so then,
What's good can be beyond what we can imagine,
Especially when change comes knocking,
The end comes knocking,
The end of something near and dear to us,
Something precious,
Change we don't want,
An end we don't want,
Maybe even something you thought you couldn't live without,

So, at this point it is to the prospect of endless possibilities you must look,
To the grandeur and the magnificence of all that is possible being possible,
New life,
New dreams,
New hopes,
New expectations,
New lessons,
New things to love,
New worlds,
New realities,
New dimensions,
Indeed, new possibilities,
So yes indeed,
When something ends,
It truly is the opportunity and possibility for something new,
Even through excruciating pain, confusion and worry,
Like when a child is born,
Labour and pregnancy end,
And new life begins,
A new universe is created,
For we are all mini universes,
Mini worlds,
Extraordinary,
Death leads to new life,
Like the carcass fertilising the ground,
Mulch,
Enriching the soil,
And new shoots spring forth from mother earth,
And even if everything died and no new life came forth,
It would be the opportunity for the most perfect silence to emerge,
An eternal silence,
Complete peace and tranquillity,

No chaos of existence to bring pain, upset or killing,
No more death,
So, the end is only the beginning,
Even when it seems it is the end of everything.

What is death when thousands die everyday?
Millions,
Animals kill,
We kill,
Kill to live,
All forms of life kill,
In war killing is permitted,
It's expected,
It's mandatory,
You can be killed for refusing to kill,
So, what is life and what is death?
We fear it,
And yet it is inevitable,
We live as if it is not,
However, it is one of the few guarantees we have in life,
We are devastated and terrified if we find out or fear we are going to die,
Or that a loved one is going to die,
Yet death frees us from the traumas and at times hellish place this life can be,
The hells of war,
The hells of violence,
The hells of murder,
The hells of hate, torture and injustice,
The hells of depression and anxiety,
The hells of jealousy and envy and the worlds they create,
The hells of domination,
The hells of poverty,
We kill for nations,
We kill to protect,
We kill for love,
We kill for hate,
So, what is death?
When it is such an everyday thing,
Such a flimsy thing,

Like some random gangland or drug cartel shooting,
What is death?
When it is the most assured thing in life,
Death,
The only way out of this heavenly and hellish place we call home,
This thing we call life,
As I lay my head to sleep,
I pray to the universe that tomorrow I wake up wiser.

1/12/22

The renewal of things,
The cycle of things,
The birth of things,
The rebirth of things,
The pain of things,
The confusion of things,
The joy of things,
The end of things,
Transition,
Transcendence,
Imagination,
Possibility,
Connection and disconnection,
Eternity and finitude,
So what is the human condition?
In light of it all,
All of it,
The wonder,
The splendour,
Obscure origins,
The many religions,
Perspectives,
Cultures,
Mythologies,
Beliefs,
What is true and what is not?
What is real and what is not?
The ethereal,
The physical,
We always seem at the brink of destruction,
Intemperate creatures,
Volatile,
Not too different from the animals we think we are superior to,
We are predatorial,
Instinctive,

Territorial,
Capable of wanton destruction,
Meaningless consumption,
Even more so today,
So what of this human race?
We fear our end,
But at the furthest reaches of space,
It's fine either way,
So what of it?
Well there's the enquiry then I say,
The juxtaposition of everything and nothingness
A beautiful symmetry
We think it all matters,
When the deepest beauty is
Well, it doesn't,
And perhaps that is what it is to be alive,
To fear the possibility of death,
For it is possible in any instant,
Presumably to the ant here on the ground,
It matters not if us humans are here or not,
Probably for the better for them,
To the farthest star away from us,
Perhaps too it doesn't matter whether us humans here are alive or not,
So why do we fight so much?
Kill,
Not cooperate meaningfully in totality,
All this just to say,
What is the human condition,
And what of it?
What is the greatest vision of ourselves we can live inside of?
Considering we are all going to die anyway.

3/12/22

Why must I feel sad,
Even in times of happiness,
Sadness creeps in like a wondering lost ghost,
Yet I realise that as the sun rises and sets,
The tide comes in and goes out,
Night becomes day,
Day becomes night,
I do traverse between the light and the dark,
Between the forces that push and the forces that pull,
I too follow the patterns of nature,
The patterns of the universe,
I am the universe,
At times my sadness is mild like a gentle breeze,
And at times deep and haunting like dark clouds before a thunderous storm,
The emotions as erratic and volatile as the weather patterns we live under,
What is within,
Certainly is without,
I am the Universe.

8/12/2022

One should not live in fear,
Rather,
One should live in unyielding rebellion to all the dark forces
that could encloud you,
Be they forces from within or forces from without,
Especially, ones that seem the most insurmountable,
That's the true spirit,
The spirit of a fearless warrior,
For to be a fearless warrior is not to be without fear,
It is to act in spite of fear,
The spirit of a soaring eagle,
A warrior who will face the foe and fight the good fight,
And the eagle that will soar high up into the sky,
Beyond the limitations of all that drags it down,
And look down upon it with courageous scorn,
Don't be fearful of the darkness and the dark shadows,
Be unyielding.

11/12/22

The wounded animal,
Yelps and howls,
Whimpers quietly in the dark and cold,
Hoping for help,
Hoping for rescue,
A passing stranger hears the cries,
The whimpers,
Guided by the instinct to help,
He approaches,
Carefully with loving intent,
Yet despite the strangers intent,
The wounded animal begins to snarl and bare its fangs,
The story of the wounded animal,
Snarling at those who wish to show it love,
Rescue it from its pain,
Lashing out,
Biting and pushing away those who care,
The story of the wounded animal,
All it knows is pain,
And if you get too close,
It might hurt maybe even kill you,
The wounded animal,
The story of life,
Pain, love, confusion and miscommunication.

Che

The human,
In a constant battle between its own needs and those of others,
A battle between being a Saint and a devil,
The innate drives of nature and the seemingly divine aspirations of the higher mind,
A battle between saving versus killing,
Survival versus death,
What a struggle,
Perhaps a beautiful struggle,
The seesaw of life,
Which side outweighs the other,
The human story,
For the individual ,
For the whole.

The lost sheep,
Lost without a shepherd,
Lost from its flock,
Wondering in the wilderness aimlessly scared and lonely,
Exposed to the dangers,
The long fanged beasts that lurk in the shadows,
Ready to pounce on defenceless prey,
With its snow white woolly fur,
 Innocent and fragile,
Lost without a shepherd,
Lost without its flock,
The Lost sheep,
Bleating hopefully in the dead of night.

12/12/22

What is love?
Just chemical reactions in the body?
Or just a deep bond governed by self-interest?
Is it a metaphysical, spiritual or supernatural phenomenon?
Some kind of cosmic manifestation beyond our comprehension,
All the great sages and teachers have spoken about it,
We obsess about it,
But what is it really?
For you can have what seemingly to us is true love for those close to you,
But not share it for those who you deem separate,
As seems to be the case for most of us,
So what is it?
What is it?
What is it?

18/12/22

A moment of clarity,
Calm serene observation,
When you become present to your being,
I am here,
In the throng of it all,
In the expanse of it all,
The extraordinarily wide expanse,
The extent of it all,
Yet located here,
In this solitary spot,
In this moment in time,
A solitary consciousness ,
A microcosm in the macrocosm,
Significant yet insignificant,
Relative to the totality if it all,
Yet I am here,
I am really here,
Surrounded but all that surrounds,
Being all that I am,
Inside of all that is,
I am alive,
What an extraordinary epiphany.

19/12/22

Little Moroccan girl,
Oh how you broke my heart,
Walking the street,
In the dead of night,
Begging strangers for money
How you held my hand
And spoke in a language I couldn't understand,
Begging,
Leave her they said,
Let's go,
This is Morocco they said,
It happens all the time,
You see it everywhere,
Just learn how to say you have no money in Moroccan,
And she'll leave you alone,
But that won't solve the problems of her world,
That won't solve the problems in the world,
If I learnt how to say I have no money in her language,
Oh how I wanted to help you,
How I wanted to give you everything I had,
You touched my soul,
You broke my heart,
You were so small,
So vulnerable,
Only yay high,
Seemingly blind,
All I could think is,
How could it be so?
How could it be so?
How could this be your fate?
Little girl,
To walk the streets at night ,
Going from stranger to stranger,
How you touched my soul,
Is this all humanity can do?

Is this all we are?
Can we do more?

22/12/22

I am a non-existent phenomenon,
Existing in an unquantifiable reality.

The human condition,
These things,
These apparitions,
In the vastness of space,
Such strange creatures,
Peculiar creatures,
Nationality,
Cultural,
Language, boundaries and barriers,
Existing,
Co Existing,
Semi co Existing,
Intelligent and dumb,
Dumb and intelligent,
Intelligent and dumb.

28/12/22

A man is a man,
Just a man,
To claim to be more is foolish
To claim to be less is dim-witted,
But he is just a man,
A man can be lost,
And a man can be found,
In the wilderness of life,
A man can truly be lost,
But we must know it in all our hearts,
That we all too can be lost,
Lost on the path of life,
Lost on the path we should have taken,
The path we would have chosen if the choice was just ours,
If everything was in our control,
Every event,
Every reaction,
But that's not life,
Not this life,
So the path you walk is the path you walk,
And a man is just a man,
No more,
No less.

29/12/22

The land,
The land,
The land,
We are nothing without the land,
You are nothing without land,
The land,
When they came and took the land they took everything,
One's own ability to look after themselves,
Not even the basics,
And it was a different relationship they sought with the land,
For the aboriginals lived with the land,
Revered the land,
And for this they were called primitive,
Yet the conqueror sought to exploit the land for wealth,
For so called human progress,
What a thought,
Human progress,
For is a person not living within their means,
In reverence and balance their surroundings progressed?
Deep in the wisdom that mother nature is looking after them,
As much as they are looking after her,
You must consume and leave enough for tomorrow,
For tomorrow stretches as far as the imagination,
Or is it the one rushing helter-skelter at a rate of knots on a wanton path to somewhere anywhere?
Maybe even their own doom,
Yet it is the 21st century,
And capitalism for the most part rules,
Capitalism won,
So, maybe that is the progress of humankind,
And to lament is a fool's errand,
Yet it remains true to say,
The land,
The land ,
The land,

And if the African must catch up,
They must teleport into the 21st century,
And discover the exploitative and productive alchemy that the
European discovered that saw them conquer the whole world.

6/1/23

Kura uone,
Grow up and see,
The greatest African proverb,
The deepest African proverb,
A short phrase,
Betraying and promulgating the deepest wisdom,
That portends the reality of life,
How with the accumulation of years,
Reality can and will come and shutter the innocence of your youth,
The thin veil that shields you in the blissfulness of youth from all life can bring,
The safety of not knowing,
Peel away at the perceived layer of protection that should envelope you in your childhood days,
Kura uone
When the tragedies of life bring themselves to bear,
Death,
Disease,
Heart break,
The inequity of life,
The malaise,
The putrid miasma of life at times which seems inescapable like the snare of a skilled hunter,
Kura uone,
Grow up and see,
Does anyone go through unscathed,
We all seemingly carry some pain,
Some tragedy,
Some complexity,
Kura uone,
Grow up and see,
A simple phrase,
Two words,
Like a binary code,

Revealing all of life's programming in one short phrase,
The algorithm of life,
The deepest phrase,
The deepest proverb,
That betrays the truth that,
Inevitably, the innocence of youth is reaped from you,
Some sooner than others,
And life bares its brutality,
So all there is to do is to grow up and see,
Face the inevitable with courage, strength and wisdom,
Kura uone,
Grow up and see,
No one escapes unscathed,
The wisdom of the ages,
Kura uone,
An axiom,
An adage.

7/1/23

The many dimensions of human existence,
Theoretical physicists and thinkers postulate on the nature of reality,
Are there other dimensions?
Other realities out there,
Yes maybe,
But I venture to say there are,
And we experience them every day in the process of being human,
We are constantly shifting between planes,
Levels of perception,
Modes and state of being,
Who you are at work and at home,
How you are when you are happy, sad or depressed,
Optimistic or pessimistic,
Reality is tangibly different,
The world you see when you travel abroad if you're privileged enough to be able to,
Seeing other cultures,
Experiencing other cultures,
Your politics,
Your social circles,
Your educational background,
Your social class,
Your economic privilege,
All different dimensions and universes unto themselves,
Even the dream state versus the awake state,
For dreams can be as vivid, enlivening or chilling as any experience in the apparent wake state,
And in a mental health crisis such as psychosis,
The boundary between worlds is well and truly ruptured,
The boundary between realities,
Seemingly so,
The mind, spirit, soul, brain, or whatever is responsible for earthly perceptions is gone elsewhere,

Yet the physical body is here in this earthly plane causing all sorts of havoc,
To some it may be called crazy,
Losing your mind,
Other modalities say it is a transpersonal experience,
Yet more spiritual outlooks might point to something more divine,
It's all about perspective and culture in the end,
Either way,
What a phenomenon,
All here,
The grandest experience is the everyday experience,
We seek for experimental and hypothetical concepts and ideas,
When it's all happening right in front of us,
What you are looking for is always right in front of you they say,
All to say,
The grandest experience is perhaps the one you are already having,
The grandest realisation is being present to the majesty of the experience,
And yet we will theorise,
And look for realities beyond this one,
And so it is,
And so it is,
And it's all good,
It's all good.

After we have fought all the wars,
Done all the fighting,
Done all the killing,
And all that there is that surrounds us,
And all it is to be,
And all it is to be alive,
Life is just a process and function of breathing in and out.

CHE

I have never witnessed a sunrise,
Today I shall,
To be alive for so long,
And never have taken a moment to,
So much escapes us,
As we are caught up in the humdrum,
In the mundane,
But today I will see the sunrise,
Witness it pierce the horizon,
Initially a reddish bronze golden hue,
At the horizon,
Then the moment of emergence,
There it is,
Heaven.

Flying,
We are actually flying,
In the midst of the clouds,
The miracle of human potential,
Human capability,
Oh,
If they could see us now,
Those of yester year,
Who envied the birds,
Believed perhaps it was only their privilege,
To elevate beyond the ground,
Yet today its as common place as pebbles on the ground,
And we take it all for granted,
But the deepest contemplation,
Lays bare our inexhaustible potential,
When lead by our deepest inspiration,
Intelligence and our greatest imaginative potential.

9/1/23

Love is like a sweet fragrance in the air,
You catch a whiff and it arouses the senses,
Triggers deep innate drives,
Lingers in your perceptions,
Haunting,
Tantalising,
Inviting,
Inspiring.

CHE

Love is hope,
Hope in despair,
Hope for better things,
Hope for beauty,
Beauty in your life,
Beauty in life,
That's love.

Love is humble,
Ultimately,
Love gives way,
Love makes space,
Accommodates,
Understands,
Love looks for the deeper meaning,
The deeper meaning in all things,
The deepest meaning,
It searches for it at all times,
Love looks for peace in the face of conflict,
That's Love,
That's true love.

Love is like the strongest element,
Yet soft like the most softest silk,
Extremely durable and tough,
Yet soft to the touch,
Enduring through the most unseasonable weather and storms of life,
Dependable and strong,
The good type of strength,
Not oppressive,
Not ruthless,
Not forceful,
Firm but malleable and adaptable,
True love.

Love is letting go,
Yet loving so much that you fear to let go,
Love is letting go,
So you don't constrict or control,
Love is letting go so life can be explored,
So love is freedom,
Freedom to freely choose,
Choose and what will be will be,
That's love and that's life.

Che

To be,
All the macro phenomena that allow us to be,
Life to be,
The sun,
The moon,
The stars,
Water,
The Universe,
And the micro phenomena,
The air we can't see,
The cells,
The atoms,
And all else,
And then we are what we are.

A human is an incredible thing,
Seemingly an animal,
With all the basic needs and traits of one,
And yet, certainly, ostensibly more developed than the animals,
Capable of more complex thoughts and creations,
Making it the foremost creature on this planet,
Yet the animal seems to be at least trapped in the world of just pure instinct,
The human seems to have been given more freedom relatively,
To carry out more what looks like free will,
Though even that can be interrogated,
But certainly in the world of relativity its more free,
And so we are,
Living a life and in a world of complex thoughts,
Complex emotions,
Social systems,
Politics,
Religion,
And all else,
The human,
A deeply fascinating thing,
Deeply fascinating indeed.

10/1/23

Love is a phenomenon of action,
Love is a phenomenon of expression,
Verbal,
Physical,
Emotional,
Love is done,
Love is lived,
The instinct to run into a burning building for love.

Che

Love is acceptance,
Acceptance of it all,
And then realising the beauty and connectedness of it all,
Then realising the true power and freedom,
The true power and freedom of living in the acceptance of it all.

Life is a process of constant pruning,
Pruning and weeding,
And when you think you're done,
You only have to start again,
The garden always needs tending,
The processes of life are constant,
Hence our consistency is required,
So even when you think you have made the grandest realisation,
Sooner or later normality sets back in,
The weeds,
You descend from your peak,
And you must rise again,
Prune some more,
Weed some more,
The garden,
Till you rediscover that serenity,
Only to yet do it again,
That way you discover the truth in even deeper ways,
Then one day you are laid to rest,
To then perhaps discover in deeper and greater truths beyond the ones that reside in this realm.

Che

The individual has to satiate itself,
Yes indeed,
That's imperative and indeed good,
But ultimately our challenges are collective,
Too our existence.

The individual must be allowed freely express themselves to the fullest extent,
So long as it doesn't oppress of course,
Reach their maximal potential,
The maximum extent of what they are capable of,
Achieve and strive,
Innovate and create,
Amass,
That's the engine of human progress,
Human creativity,
Within the bounds of human collective living,
I once met a man,
Only for an instant,
And our souls spoke,
And he said something profound,
Balance is the key to life he said,
By allowing the individual to be fully expressed,
And be the be the best they can be,
All of society benefits,
No one can know the gifts within endowed.

Love is perpetuity.

The secret is to live knowing that none of it matters,
Yet it matters absolutely,
At least to us,
Then the rest of it is just a dance,
The dance of life,
And that we make it matter,
Makes our life what it is,
And it's in the balance,
Of knowing it all matters and yet it doesn't matter,
That peace exists,
And the greatest possibility and space for a beautiful life exists.

Che

The prime responsibility of the self is to the self,
Just as your own heart beats to necessitate your own survival,
Thus, you are solely responsible for your own survival and up keep,
As the calf of a wildebeest must learn to stand, walk and run within minutes of birth
Else fall prey to predators,
One must stand on their own feet and find their own way to fulfil their own potential,
Life is not for the idle,
If it is to be lived to the full,
Of course and indeed it is good to live as a group and rely on the group,
That's good community,
But all must do their part and be self-reliant first.

Self-love,
True self love,
Not the narcissistic kind of self-love,
Nor the egotistic kind of self-love,
But the self-love that reflects upon the magnitude,
The magnitude of the wonder and splendour,
The singular miracle,
That in all there is in the universe,
In all of time and space,
You exist,
You too exist,
Along with everything else that exists,
In this time,
In this space,
Your time,
Your space,
And so you should love yourself,
And thusly you should love yourself,
And consequently all things,
For they exist,
Just as you do,
That is true love,
True self love,
The grandest place to observe reality,
That you are self and you are all.

How does a man of peace win against a man of violence?
How does an honourable person win against a Machiavellian person?
How do you negotiate with those that are willing to kill to get their way?
Seems an impossible paradox,
The ways of the dark arts seem more effective and direct than those of our higher selves,
So how does good win?
Kindness and patience seem poorly matched against aggression and dominance,
The Bible contemplates this too,
As it postulates whether to take an eye for an eye,
Or turn the other cheek,
And yet Jesus was crucified and died on the cross,
Martin Luther King shot dead,
And yet their message outlasted them,
So perhaps good does win in the end,
You might just have to lose your life in the process,
Or perhaps suffer,
However the question still lingers though,
Do you turn your other cheek to Hitler?
Or a mad person,
A tyrant,
It seems sometimes life gives us no choice,
So what to do?
Certainly those who are willing to kill and connive seemingly get their way,
I suppose then all there is,
Is for those who see the light to be the light bearers,
Then the rest is this life,
Exactly as it is.

If your search is true,
Even the wrong turn can lead you to a greater truth.

All reality is,
Is, what we are filtering through our senses,
What we are filtering through based on our level of intelligence,
So what is reality really?
Well reality to an ant is different to reality to a dog,
And so on and so on,
And us too,
On a scale of intelligence and awareness,
So what do we know then?
Well we know what we know,
We know what we can know,
And Ultimately it means we know nothing,
For compared to what we know an ant knows nothing,
Well at least relatively so on a scale relative to what we know,
Except to be an ant,
So we know nothing,
Except to be human beings,
So of all the intelligence that is out there,
All the intelligence that could be out there,
To the extent of infinity,
What tremendous wonders could and do exist,
Beyond our senses,
Beyond our level of perception,
Beyond our intelligence,
An ant couldn't appreciate our highest art,
We too can't appreciate the highest art of infinite intelligence,
Oh what beauty,
Oh what majesty,
Oh what a thought,
Oh what freedom.

12/1/22

The Dichotic Dilemma,
The observation that denotes a fundamental reality of existence,
The duality of life,
How on a phenomenological level everything seems to occur in a dual or oppositional state fundamentally,
At least most things,
A significant part of our reality is predicated upon this basic observation,
Up down even with gravity,
Hot or cold,
Night or day,
Push or pull,
Life or death,
And most demonstrably so in the world of human beings,
Right or wrong,
Good or bad,
Love or hate,
God or Devil,
Black or white,
Ignorance or wisdom,
Justice or injustice,
Fair or unfair,
Past or future,
Two people can see the same thing and glean completely different conclusions from that observation,
However this phenomenon is ubiquitous,
Even in the phenomenon of male female,
The concept of duality is replete in life,
And it poses a Dilemma in our existence or Dilemmas or extremes to cope with,
Hence The Dichotic Dilemma the fabric of life,
It is the stitching of existence,
The observer versus the observed,
Alkaline versus acidic,
Heaven and hell,

Existence is a Dichotic Dilemma,
Replete with moral and philosophical questions,
Whether to be selfish or selfless,
How to be so,
Why to be so,
The victim versus the perpetrator,
The Dichotic Dilemma is the fundamental observation of reality,
An inference into its deepest meaning,
For us,
An appreciation of its deepest paradoxes such as why are we alive if we die in the end?
And questions such as if God loves us why does God let us suffer?
And opens up a whole new world,
In the observation of all reality,
Where one can appreciate the interplay within all,
Extricate themselves from their attachment to points of view and fixed realities,
Extricate themselves from bias,
Extricate themselves from attachment to limitation,
See the connectedness of it all,
Push pull,
Nothing is in opposition ultimately though seemingly,
It's all in synchrony so life can exist,
The Dichotic Dilemma,
The other side of the looking glass,
Where reality is illuminated ,
Disentangled,
You are untangled from your emotions,
You are in the world of observation,
As untangled as you can be as an emotional creature,
The Dichotic Dilemma,
A window into an alternate perspective,
A freeing perspective.

Life on a spiritual path,
Is a process of deepening the enquiry,
Deepening understanding,
This is life on any fulfilling path,
The path to self-actualisation,
The path to mastery,
The path to wisdom.

It's in the not knowing that life exists,
That suffering exists,
If you knew what it was all for,
Then the experience will be diminished,
But we are given snippets of the truth,
Depending on what you believe,
But if we knew it all,
There would be no point to life,
Why does a baby have to die?
At the highest level of awareness,
The baby hasn't died,
Just changed states,
But down here where we exist,
At the lower states of consciousness,
Where we are attached to life as we must to live,
It is beyond a tragedy,
It is unimaginable pain,
Hence, it's in the not knowing where life exists,
The not knowing and attachment,
For if you truly knew and accepted that nothing dies and I don't need to be attached to the pain of it,
Then our life here as we know it wouldn't be possible.

You can't control other human beings because you think you know best,
That is a sin,
Every human being is a sovereign entity,
A universe of ideas,
A universe in their own right,
That kind of control leads to oppression, repression and worse,
Hence it is better to listen than to speak.
Just because people do things differently,
Doesn't make it wrong,
A mosaic is only beautiful because of all the different coloured tiles
Human differences are our mosaic.

14/1/22

Che

We are all making it up,
Yes instinct,
Yes social conditioning,
But ultimately we are all making it up,
We all make it up in our minds,
And make it mean what we make it mean,
But it's not true,
It's not reality,
It's all what we are making up,
So the real reality,
Is you can make up whatever you want,
True freedom.

15/1/22

Dear young Iranian lady shot in the eye by the regime,
I am sorry,
I thought I had suffered in my life,
But I've never lost an eye,
Not to injustice,
And I hope I never have to,
You lost your eye because you dared to propose,
Dared to suggest how you may want to live your life,
Which should be your sovereign right,
Every human should be sovereign,
Is sovereign,
At the highest level of how it ought to be,
Yet we live on earth,
And others deem their views, opinions and legitimacy supersedes others',
However,
Despite losing your eye,
And the adversity,
The threats,
You came out and showed your scars to the world,
Showed your beauty,
The beauty of your physical form,
The beauty of your spirit,
You look even more beautiful without the eye,
Because you are more than just a missing eye,
You are human,
Despite the prospect of further reprisal,
You are undaunted,
The true beauty of what it is to be alive,
Of being human,
That even standing at the end of the barrel of a gun,
We charge,
We charge in defiance,
Charge in the face of tyranny,
For how long will with those with power abuse it?
An ode to all oppressed people.

Poetry,
The art of writing,
The art of turning words into representations of life,
Not just melody, rhyme and abstraction,
But a deep dive into the soul,
The art of expressing our deepest feelings,
Connecting with life dreams and hopes,
Painting a canvas of life but with words,
A way to critique society, life and the world,
A way to inspire,
A way to analyse but with flowery imagination,
Not bland and prosaic,
Poetry,
The language of the heart through the creativity of the mind in words,
Perhaps even our connection to the universe in words.

17/1/22

Could earth be paradise?
Certainly it's all here,
Demonstrably so,
All things ugly and all things beautiful,
We can be in heavenly states and hellish states of emotion,
We don't have to wait for some fanciful afterlife,
It's all here,
So could earth be paradise?
And what would it take?
Oh, our capabilities are tremendous,
Indeed animals can build beautiful structures,
Like the beehive,
And the Ant hills,
But my, does the human excel,
From the pyramids of yesteryear,
And the cathedrals and castles of the world,
The stone monuments,
But in this day,
The mighty sky scrapers of the modern city scape,
The unbelievable bridges across seas and rivers which defy imagination and seemingly what's humanly possible,
The great dams, Hoover and Kariba and such,
To be so endowed yet so strangely self-sabotaging
Yes we know it's the Dichotic Dilemma but can we not transcend it?
Modern science,
Modern medicine,
The machines,
Mobile technology,
Satellites,
The most rapid technological acceleration in a split second of cosmic time,
A nano second in time,
For its not too long ago,
Just over a century the world was pitch black,

Covered in darkness,
Now we have instantaneous lighting,
Instantaneous communication,
And the most complex Web of interconnectedness yet,
Seems paradise is desperately trying to manifest,
Subconsciously that's what we are trying to manifest,
To conquer our environment and limitations and live well,
Technology is such a powerful tool yet over reliance on it seems risk laden and ill fated,
But that's by the by,
What's evident,
Is our ability to create,
Our seemingly incredible potential,
We have penetrated space,
Sent probes to further reaches of space,
And the space race is only a recent phenomenon,
So could earth be paradise?
Well,
It seems we can achieve and do anything we want,
And yet conquering yourself and your limitations is perhaps the toughest battle,
They do say the greatest battle is the battle with oneself,
When humanity sees that,
Then maybe that's the epiphany,
It's one organism,
It might have different organs but the fundamental elements are the same,
And ultimately its one body,
So could earth be paradise?
Well,
I as a writer can only posit the question,
Point to the possibility,
And posit the aspiration.

Life is beautiful,
It is really,
When the emotions sore,
To a crescendo,
When in a moment of bliss,
Surrounded by loved ones or ecstasy,
How is that not beautiful?
How beautiful is that?
The possibility of it,
How we persevere,
How we try to make it work,
Overcome our limitations,
How we are blinded,
Blinded from infinity,
But we still strive for greatness,
Strive to survive,
How we are shielded from wisdom,
But we still are,
How is that not beautiful?

Che

Peace is being right at the center of it all,
At the center of the extremes,
All that you hate and all that you love,
Being at the center of how you think the world should be and how it shouldn't be,
And not wishing that it should be any other way,
But accepting that it is the way it is,
That is the platform,
The point of peaceful creation,
Not adversarial creation,
Hateful creation,
For we are creating life in every moment,
Every step we take,
Every word we utter,
Every intention we have.

The reality of it is,
In all that's negative about human existence,
The toxicity,
The death,
The chaos,
There are miracles,
True miracles within the same reality,
Awe inspiring phenomena,
Like love,
From smallest to the greatest expression of it,
It is a truly awe inspiring phenomena,
And it's good to believe in the good things,
Indeed,
Love,
A phenomena as awe inspiring as creation itself.

Che

The more you forgive,
The more you see,
Then the more you see,
The more you forgive,
So forgive,
And you will see,
And when you see,
See more clearly,
It's all better.

The lowest form of debate,
The lowest form of discourse,
Is to assume that everything your fellow is saying,
Is wrong.

Indeed the resolution for humanity,
Is a philosophical one,
Ultimately,
How we perceive ourselves in relationship to each other,
Is it possible to live under an overarching definition,
And still retain the identities we hold so dear,
The identities we use to define ourselves as separate at times,
Rather than as a reflection,
Perhaps as that of light glimmering off the surface of a polished diamond,
The different manifestations of the being human,
Isn't that why diamonds are so coveted,
Because of the way they refract light into a polychromatic spectacle,
H L Mencken said that love is the triumph of imagination over intelligence,
A truly profound insight,
Intelligence being the beast that must survive and so it claws,
Imagination being the unbridled possibility of all that is,
The key to untold realities and presently unimaginable things,
So what is the limit of our imagination?
What is the greatest philosophical appreciation of ourselves and our interconnectedness,
Interrelation and interdependence that we can make?
And so it is.

It must be said,
The invention of racism,
For that's what it was,
Was and is one of the greatest stains on human reality,
Indeed humans devalue each other at times outside of the context of racism,
However, there was something particularly pernicious about racism,
Enduring and truly dehumanising,
How whole institutions and an intellectual class was created to promulgate and maintain the idea,
What a powerful force,
And indeed what a powerful force to undo,
A force that legitimises so much,
Infects so much,
And limits so much,
And alas,
An observation it is.

Che

It's the serendipity of it all,
If you give it time,
If you are patient,
Through the sadness,
Through the confusion,
Perhaps the heartbreak and loneliness,
The dark times,
When it's time,
Like a supernova,
A sudden burst of cosmic light,
Radiant and magnetic,
Love strikes,
All of a sudden,
From nowhere,
Like cupids arrow,
Instantaneously, reality is illuminated,
A new age begins,
Within the vicinity of that explosion,
The explosion in your heart,
New love,
Love.

18/1/23

The paradox is,
That one word,
Immigrant,
Worse yet,
Illegal Immigrant,
Conjures up so much,
So much bile for the hateful angry politician,
The hateful angry nationalist,
Perhaps even racist,
At least some are,
Perhaps it's unfair to call them hateful and angry,
Apparently they just want to secure their borders,
They just want orderly migration,
Not too many people to dilute the indigenous population,
Perhaps for a romantic idealist it's simple and about humanity,
But perhaps to a realist there are relevant and pragmatic issues,
Perhaps both are true and indeed probably are,
In any case the angry headlines persist,
The vociferous incessant press articles,
The controversy,
The worsening rhetoric,
What a broken world,
The amazing thing about what's missed in all the anger,
Is the individual story of those Immigrants,
Those illegal Immigrants,
The intrinsic humanity within them,
The dreams and aspirations they carry,
The sacrosanct humanity,
That individual spark,
What is it worth?
An invasion they say,
Let's turn the boats away,
Let's reduce the numbers,
However,

They never really want to spend too much time asking what the root causes of all this apparent mayhem are,
Perhaps facing the real truth in the eye is too daunting,
They would rather scapegoat,
All kinds of arguments abound,
Yet I say the real problem is a lack of imagination,
It's clear enough to see that if people don't have reason to move or leave they wouldn't,
So why can't we work towards that?
However, what's even more imaginative,
Is that in the most perfect world,
Everyone would be able to go where they want and live where they find contentment,
Regardless of who they are.

Che

We all live in hope,
We must live in hope,
Hope keeps us alive,
Hope keeps us optimistic,
Especially through the worst of times,
And even in the best of times,
So to live without hope,
You might as well be dead,
Hope is the undying flame of life.

If your initial assumption is that you know it all,
Or have all the answers,
Then you are already irrevocably lost.

Inspiration is communication with a higher intelligence,
Distilling the truth from a higher source into our reality,
Creating from beyond our realm to the realm of the living,
That's why true inspiration is so awe inspiring,
Seemingly unbelievable,
So captivating,
Life changing,
Seemingly impossible to imagine,
Impossible to replicate,
Because its beyond our realm.

Love sets the highest bar,
It is what we aspire for,
And reality is the test to whether we can reach that bar or maintain it,
Love is a state of absolute perfection and reality is a dynamic chaotic state,
Ultimate love is absolute equilibrium,
A balance between your expectations and their expectations,
And of course the shared manifestation of the euphoric feeling of love,
Seemingly though,
Humanity can only postulate on the highest ideals and perhaps most times cannot reach or maintain them,
That is what it is to be human,
But if you can feel true love or the possibility of it even for a short while,
Then that's a really good thing.

Che

Everything is an exchange of energy,
There is a price to be paid for everything,
To be successful you must generally work very hard and be determined,
That's the price to pay that's the exchange of energy,
To hate you must be consumed by a lot of ill will and negative feeling,
That's the price you pay, that's the exchange of energy,
To love you must be very caring, compassionate, patient, thoughtful and many other good and trying things,
That's the price you pay, that's the exchange of energy,
To be lazy and idle you must be uninspired and largely live a meaningless existence,
That's the price you pay, that's the exchange of energy,
To be intelligent or wise you must think a lot, reflect a lot, critique a lot, analyse a lot and be deeply insightful,
Which can take a lot of time, attention and be very consuming,
That's the price you pay, that's the exchange of energy,
To really love your child, generally your concerns have to become secondary,
That's the price you pay, that's the exchange of energy,
To live you must aspire and expire,
That's the price you pay, that's the exchange of energy.

Everyone believes they are doing good,
Even those who are doing bad as it were,
Believe they are doing good,
By whatever narrow limited or misguided lense they are viewing from,
Fundamentally they believe they are doing good,
Hence one can posit that the fundamental motivation of the human is to be good,
What then makes it bad is the impact it has on others,
Then the good bad duality can exist or comes into play,
But the fundamental drive of the individual is to be good,
Hence you must believe in the goodness in all,
That allows you to see it in the first instance,
Whatever little there is in some instances perhaps,
That's a start,
And that's wisdom,
It also gives you the possibility to draw it out,
Or draw it out more for those who are misguided,
But the foundation is to believe that everyone is good,
The only concern is scope and misguidance,
Whatever thing they are serving,
They believe it to be good,
Even the most diabolical,
The oppressors of the day,
Think they are the saviours,
And so it has been,
And so it may continue being,
And so it is.

True enlightenment is living at the edge of what's possible and what's impossible,
True mastery is living at the edge of what's possible and what's impossible,
True wisdom is being intrinsically ensconced between the extremities of ignorance and clarity,
And know that one is only the path to the other,
True intelligence is seeing the unity and interconnectedness of it all yet being present to the distinctions,
The individual is the whole,
And the whole is the individual,
There is no whole without the individual,
And there is no individual without the whole,
Without everything else,
You don't exist.

Let's follow a reductionist pathway shall we,
So if I am an individual ,
But I'm also the whole,
And the whole cannot exist without the individual,
And the individual cannot exist without the whole,
What if I was the only thing that was in existence?
Would I then exist?
Well the answer is no,
Because to exist there must be other things that are not you,
So you can know you are not them,
Then you can know or at least invent what you are,
We generate reality or observe reality in our minds by there being an external reality out there,
I know I'm not a tree because I'm different to a tree,
So for me to exist as human in this instance as distinct to a tree,
A tree must exist,
So without an external world out there,
You cannot be,
You are a void,
There is no stimulus coming in to give you being,
No light,
No smell,
No touch,
No sight,
You couldn't generate thought,
You couldn't generate speech,
You couldn't create,
So the question then is,
What if I was an entity in existence but in isolation and able to create independent of an external objective reality?
Independent of there being other things,
To create where there is nothing else other than me,
Just my mind,
Well then,
You would be God,

CHE

An entity that can create out of nothing,
Generate reality for itself where there is no reality,
You would be God,
For you would need the omnipotence and the omniscience,
The omnipotence to be able to have the power to create,
And the omniscience to be able to imagine any reality you wanted and fill it with whatever you want,
You would be God,
A God,
Whether you think that God is a conscious mind for the spiritualists,
Or a particle for the materialists,
You would be some kind of generative omnipotent, omniscient entity,
The irony of it however,
The grand realisation,
At least in this ode,
Is that that's exactly what we are,
That's exactly what we are doing,
Generating and creating reality in our minds,
As mini gods on earth,
We are made in God's image it is said,
We are God's children,
Demonstrably so.

19/1/23

This poet loves all,
This poet has learnt to love all,
This poet has learnt the value of love,
This poet is still learning the fullest value of true love,
Because this poet is human,
And he is limited,
So the fullest extent of true love,
Is beyond his intelligence,
His imagination,
To this poet,
The truest extent of love,
Is at the level of infinite intelligence,
And infinite intelligence,
Is beyond our capacity,
All this to say,
This poet is a black man,
And it's incumbent upon him to reflect on the black story,
This poet knows though ultimately he is not just limited to this,
But this is the context of our existence,
His existence,
And still has significant relevance,
To a lessening extent,
But still to a notable extent,
Notable enough that it must be addressed,
And it's on this basis the poet says these words below,
Black person,
They said you were unintelligent,
Don't make it true,
Black person they said you were predisposed to violence and crime,
Don't make it true,
Black person they said if you take over the reins of power there would be untold ruin,
Don't make it true,
Black person they said you're gangsters and thugs,

Don't make it true,
Black person they said you stab and shoot,
I say to you,
Implore you to put the knives and the guns down,
Youth and some grown men alike with your trousers below your waistline exposing your under garments,
Perhaps pull your trousers up and buckle them properly,
Don't be a caricature,
Don't be what someone who wants the worst for you wants you to be,
Ultimately despite the prevailing winds the integrity of the human still remains within your remit,
Black person you are largely emancipated around the world,
Grab the reins of destiny,
Be the greatest version of yourself you could possibly be,
Be what your most unfettered imagination wants you to be,
Break free,
Only because at one point you were wilfully, powerfully and systematically denied this,
Black person, don't be a victim,
For your victimhood becomes a self-restraining chain holding you down,
Realise your own agency,
Acknowledge your own power to hurt,
For that is what it is to be human,
Victor Frankl noted that even in the most adverse circumstances your mind can be your refuge,
And within that you can create anything,
They said you have no culture Black person no history,
Well you can create a culture of excellence,
Just as the Germans are known for efficiency,
The black person can be known for excellence,
Make a new history black person,
And not be defined by a history of chains and colonisation,
Make a new history,

Make a new history,
It's in your hands,
However, I also assure you that you had a great history as any human group,
But now you must cease your future,
Be undeterred for you were deterred,
Be inspired for you were told not to dream,
You were told your dreams didn't matter,
Your dreams could not be reality,
You were prevented from dreaming,
You were prevented from learning,
Told your minds couldn't understand the information,
So learn like your life depends on it,
Devour every book,
Seek all knowledge,
Be proud to be intelligent,
For one day I say,
Whole institutions existed to tell you, convince you and convince themselves that you are not,
So prove them wrong,
Prove that dastardly history wrong,
Be proud to learn,
Be proud to be excellent,
It's all in your hands now,
And where it's not,
We will fight that it is.
Fight the good fight.

You can't save anyone,
Really only they can save themselves,
You're not really here to save anyone,
And if you truly believe you are here to save others,
And only you can save them,
Then you can become a tyrant.

Hate does not really exist per se,
All there is,
Is love,
Hate is a product of there being love,
It is a by-product of love,
If you hate something,
It is because you love another thing,
All hate really is,
Is a manifestation of being human,
It just helps create the human condition,
For all there is,
Is love,
And for us to experience life as we know it,
Experience polarity,
Duality,
Which creates us and them,
Me and you,
In this instance love and hate,
Then hate has to existence,
Otherwise all there is, is love
Outside of the human frame of reference,
All there is,
Is love,
All there is,
Is life.

The ability to believe everything,
To be so open minded that you can accept everything,
At the very least accept it on its merits to be observed,
Accept it without compromising your ability to be critical,
But accept it only as a way to accentuate your capacity to learn and understand,
That's the true path to enlightenment,
That is the path of the true knowledge seeker,
Not the idealogue.

Che

You should not seek knowledge,
Or pursue so called facts to prove yourself right,
To a certain extent of relativity,
Facts do not exist,
You must pursue knowledge to extend understanding,
Right and wrong in the human realm is beyond establishment for multitudinous reasons,
Too multitudinous to mention in their entirety of one ode,
All we can ever truly hope for is an incremental understanding,
And that's if our baseline assumptions were correct in the first place,
Ostensibly we can make anything work and live by whatever truth we create,
Whatever rules we create,
That is the power of creation understanding and manifestation we have been given,
But to assert that what we have concluded is the absolute truth,
That's at the very least,
Misguided.

The true leader must surround themselves with those smarter than him or her,
Wiser than him or her,
Empower them with the absolute liberty to express themselves,
Undeterred,
Unfettered,
To challenge with respect,
In a quest to make the best decisions,
For at the highest levels of power,
Every decision affects absolutely,
The true leader,
The good leader should welcome challenge,
Not sycophancy.

CHE

There is an African proverb which says,
A young child should spend as much time with its grand parent,
And the grand parent should spend as much time with the child,
Learning from each other,
Because one has just come from the truth,
And the other is just about to return,
What exquisite beauty,
What exquisite poetry,
What an appreciation of existence.

Mwana wamambo,
Muranda kumwe,
The child of a King or a Queen is a servant elsewhere,
A Shona proverb that speaks to the humility that an enlightened person should walk through life with,
No matter who you are,
Your station,
Your achievements,
Your status,
Imagine if everyone had a sense of their own limits,
And the insight to not let hubris get in the way,
What world would be possible,
Mwana wamambo,
Muranda kumwe,
And they said Africa had nothing to teach the world.

Everything that exists is exquisitely beautiful,
Chiefly by the very nature that it exists,
When it might not have,
In all that is creation,
It is exquisitely beautiful by nature of its characteristics,
It's uniqueness,
It's moment in time,
Whether it's animate,
Or inanimate,
Conscious or otherwise,
Even all that we think has no consciousness,
Is just a matter of relativity,
We think the rock lacks consciousness,
The tree lacks consciousness,
But everything is levels and degrees,
And even no consciousness is a measurable demonstrable quantity,
Which creates the paradox of possibility and impossibility,
Then everything is beyond imagination,
Or the willingness of that human to imagine or accept,
Hence, why all that is should be valued,
Respected,
As an equal constituent part of all that is,
For we just don't know,
All this to say,
The deepest sense of appreciation,
Creates the most awe inspiring beauty,
Even just as a point of reference,
And in the end,
That's all your existence is,
A point of reference,
Then one day you leave this plane,
So in this moment of clarity does it not demonstrate the sheer ignorance of racism, jingoism, tribalism and all those diminished things,
And so it is,
What point of reference will you choose?

Life is an epic tale to see what you are made of,
You can be as wise as you want to be,
As ignorant as you want to be,
As evil and corrupt as you want to be,
Truly evil,
Truly corrupt,
To the furthest extent of it,
Or as kind and loving as you can be,
As benevolent,
Or as malevolent,
That's true freedom,
Or at least the freedom we are given as human beings,
The freedom to take life or preserve it,
Value it or detest it,
Value others or detest them,
Be just or unjust,
We can be it all,
In this life,
That's why no one really can be the judge of the other,
Because no one begins and ends without erring,
To err is to be human,
The imperative is to err learn grow and not repeat,
This is why as humans we can reflect,
And if you think you do not err,
You are probably erring the most.

20/1/23

Democracy can be chaotic,
But it's freedom,
At least that's its fundamental tenet,
Freedom and the accountability of power,
This is truly sacrosanct for the absence of this,
I propose is a worser evil,
When everyone has a voice,
Can have a say,
It can create a mighty mess,
Noise and clamour,
Slow progress,
But sometimes slow progress is a good thing,
And yet other times it might not be,
Thats why perhaps the best safeguards for a healthy democracy,
Are an informed and participant electorate,
Hence, why we need to uphold truth and honesty in the offices of power,
And most importantly in the media that informs the public,
Disseminates information on a mass scale,
Democracy is the best choice this poet asserts and the best invention we've made in the political structures we have,
We are hierarchical creatures,
Some form of overarching power structure must exist in society,
And a power structure with unrecallable, unaccountable, permanent power is not optimal comparatively,
Democracy has its drawbacks like anything we can create,
I fear perfection might be impossible for us,
We can only hope for the closest thing,
Thus, to have freedom, and an accountable and recallable power structure,
Those draw backs are worth having,
It is said absolute power corrupts absolutely,
And our existence is replete with examples to this end,
Hence in our world,
Democracy.

Find the God within yourself,
And by that it's to say,
Fight the good within yourself,
Find the light,
Search for the light,
That's the true path of light,
From darkness to the light,
From ignorance to bliss,
Ultimately it's a personal journey,
Don't look for external saviours,
Others may lead you astray,
Not have the best interests for you,
Be charlatans,
Be thieves and crooks,
Of course one should learn and borrow from the wisdom of others,
Their intelligence and those who've walked the road before them,
But the journey is yours,
The quest is yours,
The enlightenment you seek is your enlightenment,
Not someone else's enlightenment,
Just as you can take the donkey to the water,
But you can't force it to drink,
No one can make you see,
What you can't see for yourself,
Don't be a sheep,
Seek your own enlightenment,
And be one with it all.

Justice is about making recompense to the losses of the victim,
Whatever they may be,
Against the highest collective ideals of humanity,
By that, it's to say even the offender has rights,
And should be dealt with within the strictures of civility,
This allows for cohesion and not anarchy,
True justice then can only exist in a system where all the necessary assets for it to exist, exist,
A trustworthy judiciary,
A trustworthy legal system,
A trustworthy law enforcement system,
A trustworthy political system,
So the true course to as just an outcome as possible is possible.

Che

Perhaps the secret to life,
Is to have the right level of empathy,
Such that you are kind,
But the right level of objectivity,
Such that you are rational when faced by life's complex conundrums,
Rationality being the ability to calmly, effectively and maybe even quickly make important decisions if needs must,
All rooted in a fundamental moral and ethical foundation,
You must know who you are,
So that when the tempest comes,
And it will,
You're not found lost all out at sea.

Wisdom is the highest form of intelligence,
In the realm of humanity,
Wisdom is the ability to be critical, insightful, deeply analytical, reflective and balanced,
And that's why Wisdom brings you to the best conclusion humanely possible,
Because this ode asserts that it is the highest form of intelligence,
For a truly wise person might know how to build a nuclear weapon,
But may most likely choose not to,
You can be so intelligent you figure out the secrets of the universe and be a brigand,
Then that's not the highest form of intelligence,
That intelligence is a risk to us all.

CHE

There is nothing true in the realm of humanity,
It is all made up,
There is apparent physicality and form,
And yes that gives us an access to observe and extrapolate,
It gives us consistency,
And on that basis we can make working ideas,
But that doesn't make it truth,
It makes it true within the boundaries of our ability to understand,
If we were infinitely and unlimitedly intelligent,
Then perhaps our conclusions and insights would be true,
The Truth,
Physical form is our access to some level of truth,
That's why modern technology and science work and knowledge that has existed in the past,
Everything else is inspiration and imagination which cannot be proven,
So laugh politely in the face of someone who thinks they know it all,
Or acts as though they do.

Ultimately in life it's not about the answers you find,
You can prove anything you want,
Consequently, it's about the questions you ask,
And if it is about the answers,
Then it's about what you make those answers mean,
And we can make them mean anything,
Hence, ask the right questions,
That might be the better path.

CHE

There is no such thing as free will per se,
At least not for us,
Not in this plane of instinct, conditioning and reaction,
All we have is degrees of awareness,
And the more aware you are,
The more you can influence your intentions,
Thus your actions thoughts or beliefs,
And that's at the very least,
What we can call free will,
But true free will,
Is possible at the level of no pre conditions,
And that's not possible for us,
And by that measure,
We are absolved to some extent,
But not excused.

22/1/23

Don't compete,
Exist.

The conqueror creates the narrative,
The conqueror gives the labels.

CHE

Be greater,
Be greater than it all,
Especially the small things,
Care only for the greatest things,
The rest,
Just be in the presence of existence,
And be polite and kind.

Hitler is not an anomaly,
He lives in all of us,
Jesus is not an anomaly,
He lives in all of us,
Buddha is not an anomaly,
He lives in all of us,
Martin Luther King Jr is not an anomaly,
He lives in all of us.

Che

Life is that great conundrum,
Where everything is possible,
In every extent,
In infinite directions,
In infinite ways,
And here you find yourself,
Human being.

Thank you again for reading my book and I say again in the hope that you have read my previous books.

I'll make an admission as a way of a conclusion. I write for many reasons. For the expressive joy of it. To deepen my spiritual understanding and connection with what is. I write to sublimate, to create and maybe even to entertain. However, at the very inception of my journey into writing when the world was a truly evil and horrible place in my younger days, I was faced by a quandary. As a member of the black race and living on the African continent we seemed oppressed and quite frankly oppressed worldwide.

Hence, growing up a lot of the historical figures that had taken up the fight for our liberation or betterment were either killed or faced great challenges fighting the system that was oppressing us. The likes of Martin Luther King Jr, Steve Biko, Malcolm X, Nelson Mandela et Al. The list is inexhaustible and many people that will never make the pages of a history book.

Consequently, as a young man who was spirited about making a difference I had to ask myself, why do people who want to change the world or make a difference get killed or have to suffer greatly. Maybe it was cowardice, and maybe it was a reflection on the trauma it might inflict on those who care about you or maybe it just seemed unjust and it was a challenge to the universe.

I then had to figure out how I could change or influence the world to see the changes I believed in and contemplated politics but it looked like an unsavoury game to me. Especially in Africa or despotic places of the world or anywhere really where you can pay with your life for your political position. I don't believe in war or fighting so I couldn't be an insurgent of some description so all there was left really is just to write and hope that the influence of my words would have the desired effect.

So, what do I want? I guess what Che Guevara and most fair-minded people wanted and want. To live in a fair and just world where everyone is okay. It surely isn't a bad ideal or aspiration to have. I suppose at this stage it's apt to add that a lot of my writings in this book as in my first poetry book veered beyond just poetry or poetic and philosophical musings but to spiritual assertions. This is because at some level I believe that fundamentally, the salvation of humanity is only possible through a spiritual awakening or understanding. I don't think we will necessarily solve our problems in the political arena. Without being too scathing it seems prone to and can be a den of skulduggery. After all Machiavelli is dubbed in some circles the father of modern day politics. Tells you all you need to know really.

We certainly won't solve our problems through the arena of war. I also don't think religion as it manifests today and has manifested is the answer either. I won't speak against religion beyond that as I know it's a sacrosanct matter for those thus entwined. However, I do believe that the salvation of humanity is spirituality. An understanding of our connectedness to the universe and each other on a personal and collective level. Devoid of subdivisions and the trappings some aspects of conventional religion as we know it, respectfully. A mass awakening at every level of society to the totality of all that is and the beauty and our collective place in it all. Those are my assertions and why hence I did write some pieces which were spiritualistic postulates.

I will admit that perhaps for some and in the end, some of my musings perhaps reached an extreme level of hypothetical conjecture. However, for me that's the beauty of the imagination and the ability of the intellect to enquire. However, there was a more serious side to the extremity of the hypothesising. Just as the Founding fathers of America founded America proclaiming to uphold the highest values in the history of humanity whilst owning slaves. I believe if you are imagining or creating a possibility for humanity, you have to posit or propose the highest ideals. You have to create the greatest and highest possible ideas against all the limitations of being human. Just as the Founding fathers of America were slavers yet declaring all men are born equal. So, this is why I tried to go to the furthest extent of my imagination to propose and imagine what I hope for humanity versus all that I believe limits us. If you propose the highest beliefs or ideas in the first instance, then at least you can aspire to them or have a frame of reference when you have been pulled down into the everyday banality, mediocrity, misdirection and confusion of being human.

I would also like to say at this stage that everything I write are original musings however of course nothing is new under the sun. So, I imagine these ideas exist somewhere else in the world or through some writing. However, I haven't necessarily studied theology or philosophy. My writing journey has been an organic response to life. The only statements that haven't been my own or the external influences I have incorporated into this work have been H L Menckels assertion that love is the triumph of imagination over intelligence. I just found that to be exceptionally erudite and enlightened and so demonstrates the idea of duality and clearly demonstrates his level of appreciation of not just love and its utility but the power of the mind to think beyond our limitations. If you combine love and imagination. Wow. I also incorporated Victor Frankl in one of my poems as his book Man's search for meaning so beautifully demonstrates the idea of the mind and the human to see possibility in any circumstance. That's deeply moving and empowering. In addition, I incorporated the African proverbs I mentioned not just as part of a political ploy to undo the centuries of character assassination of the African by Western colonisers and the colonial mindset but also, because I was deeply moved by the wisdom of the statements. Furthermore, as a reflection of my ambitions to influence people's thinking in the name of positive progress for humanity, there was great utility in including them. Africa wasn't and isn't the dark continent after all with no history. I will make this point everywhere I can and with as much repetition because I believe the ultimate emancipation of the black person as the marginalised person in the world comes with the emancipation of Africa and the African mind. However, my concern for humanity doesn't just extend to black people. Just to make that abundantly clear.

Consequently then, that's why I write. A kind of soft pressure. An illumination and intrigue into the wonders of existence and a soft persuasive pressure to enlighten us on what could be possible. I am not saying I am enlightened but I am definitely saying I am enlightened to the belief and understanding that we are all human beings on this planet and ultimately all earthlings and if that was somehow some cornerstone collective ideal or belief. Who knows what could be truly possible. What was and has been most profound has been transcending the duality of right and wrong. Chiefly through a deeper appreciation of the phenomenon I first expressed in my first foray into writing, The dichotic Dilemma. Once you do that, a whole new world is possible.

Then in the end a new level of contemplation is and was possible. I'm not this human I thought I was. This black African. This story. This indignant creature. Perhaps I'm more, and now at thirty-eight, relative to when I started this writing journey with a bit more knowledge and insight, I realise and know that I certainly am just a speck if that in the universe.

I am at least a reference point and depending from what point of view you look I'm either this so called flesh, these chemicals, these particles and sub atomic particles, quantum space. Looking out I'm very small, fixed and bound with everything else beyond me. Looking in I'm infinite. My imagination is infinite. So, what am I? This thing that my parents decided to call Raleigh. That in society is something relative to others. Or am I more. At thirty-eight, I am choosing to see the more. Have learnt and searched to see the more. Against the backdrop of the absolute nonsense life can be. Utter mediocrity. To see and project the greatest possibility in my mind. To escape the meaningless and mundanity and find the extraordinary. To see the heaven in everything and not the hell. What a reference point. A reference point for the contemplation, possibility and construction of everything. The epiphany when enemies realise they were not enemies at all. They were the best of friends.

I truly know now the purpose and meaning of that philosophical question that asks, if a tree falls and there is no one present, does it make a sound. And yet the enquiry continues.

And with that.

God speed!!!

I would like to conclude the book with this final poem which I was commissioned to write on my dad's birthday by my brothers because my reputation as the writer in the family was starting to precede me.

To me it represents love which is a cornerstone belief for me and if I was religious that would be my religion. To me my father represents that. A life time of loving commitment and also evolution. My father represents all that's possible just with a loving commitment through it all. Through it all it is to be human then at the end all that's left is beauty. So....

Dad we love you,
Maybe in our younger days we might have resented how hard you were,
How firm you were,
But now we see it was your way to make us men,
Not just men but good and strong men,
We also see that it only came from love,
And it was love,
And to be around you now,
Your beautiful soul in full display,
At peace with us almost as friends almost as equals but always as sons,
It's a true blessing to have been under such stewardship,
Sir you are like the rising sun,
Dependable and reliable,
A metronome,
Consistent and constant,
You are strong,
And you have lead,
Thank you sir,
With deepest love,
Your sons .

And with that said. A special mention to my mother. The truest representation, personification and embodiment of love that I have ever met. I might say love is my religion, but its not of my doing, its because of years and years of seeing it expressed and lived out. Mum. You are an angel. Family is everything. Maybe even, the human family.

www.ingramcontent.com/pod-product-compliance
Lightning Source LLC
LaVergne TN
LVHW012057070526
838200LV00070BA/2788